Musings

of

A Mad Hungarian

A Collection of Poems on Life, Love, Loss and Hope

(Black And White Version)

Csaba Méra

Written by Csaba Mera
Art work copyright of Csaba Mera

Csaba Méra

Musings
of
A Mad Hungarian

A Collection of Poems on Life, Love, Loss and Hope

(Black And White Version)

Csaba Méra

Table Of Contents

LIFE

LOVE

LOSS

HOPE

PREFACE

Attila the Hun was one of the most powerful rulers in world history. His youngest son, Csaba, was a strong leader and skilled warrior, credited with leading the Huns to victory in every battle.

Five generations later, Arpad united and led the confederation of Magyar tribes, and is recognized as the founder of the nation of Hungary.

Csaba became a popular name for newborns as a rebuke by Hungarians to the oppression and mistreatment by the authoritarian communist rulers as a subjugated, satellite nation of the Soviet Union.

Born in his homeland of Hungary, a few years after the end of the second world war Csaba Méra (Woodenhorseboy), was raised by a nationally respected physician father and a talented mother, who left her successful acting and singing career to care for the family.

At age two years, Csaba almost died of a disease yet unidentified at the time later, known as a hemolytic uremic syndrome. At age seven, he escaped with his mother and younger brother, fleeing to Austria in the middle of the night, as the Soviets crushed the 1956 Hungarian revolution.

His father had left earlier to prepare for what was to come. The family was reunited in Austria and was accepted on the British refugee quota in early 1957.

Throughout elementary school and grammar school in Great Britain, he struggled with the new language, new customs and trying to be accepted. Csaba went to High school in Canada and went to college in the US- this led Csaba to medical school to fulfill his dream of following in his father's footsteps to becoming a doctor.

These poems are Csaba's reflections on the complexities of many events, feelings, and dreams over the decades of his life. Drawn from his experiences as a refugee, foreigner, physician, husband,father, teacher, and a humble student of life, Csaba presents his observations on an expansive, complex emotional journey.

Along the way, he has referred to himself as The Mad Hungarian. Mad about life and all its messy complications. Mad about all the goodness, caring and love he has encountered along the way. And mad about trying to understand and empathize with the struggles and losses that so many people experience in their lives on our pale blue dot.

Hoping these poems elicit a smile, an occasional chuckle, a few tear drops, and some sincere considerations about the many nuances of life, love, loss, and hope.

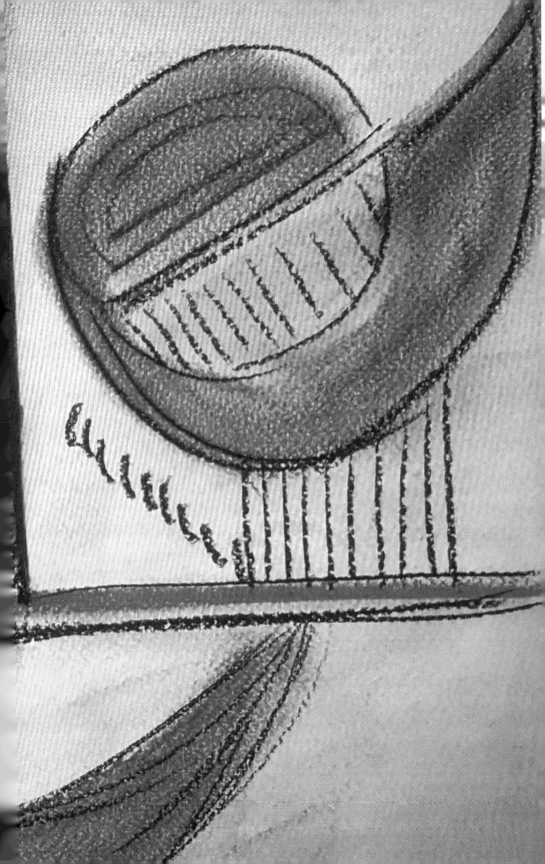

LIFE

ATTILA IS BORN

on a silvery-clouded evening
he is on his way
black hair glistening
as his round head insinuates itself
through the portal of the birth canal

oblivious to the agonal moans of his mother
his head pushes out
between her taught trembling thighs

eyes shut
face squashed
covered with vernix and blood
he makes his entrance into

THE WORLD

the midwife vigorously wipes
debris from his face
pries open his mouth
swabs the bloody fluid from within
as his face registers painful grimaces

his head is lifted upward
pulling his left shoulder
over the bloody split flesh
of his mother's vulva

then his head is pulled down
with more effort this time
allowing his right shoulder to free itself
from under his mother's pubic bone

thus the largest portion of his torso
is delivered and the rest of him is out
in a lunge
the final dive
that newborns take
into the cold uncaring world
into the tenuousness of

LIFE

from the amniotic fluids that had
filled his lungs
surrounded him
supported him
for nine months

there is no return
no choice to stay
within the protective embrace
of his mother's womb

no one asked
whether he was ready
to face the uncertainty and perils
of life on the outside

like a drunkard awakening
in the gutter of a village street
he feels the cold air around him
it chills his flesh deep
into its sinews and bones

he kicks and struggles
screaming and gagging

as the midwife repeatedly
wipes his face and nose
swabs inside his screaming mouth
removing the final remnants
of his past environs

thus attila is born
into the world
like all other humans
but destined to become

LEGEND

ALTAR BOY

the altar boy
seven years old
may be shy
but he is bold

with confidence
he walks along
his hair is short
his surplice long

thurifer he gently swings
he spreads the incense
while the church bells ring
the altar boy obeys the rules

for they are strict and clear
they provide him all the tools
but keep him full of fear

disobedience has bad outcomes
the altar boy knows all too well
for on one occasion he discovered
that being bad could end in hell

sunday school was always held
for children in the belfry tower
the bell ropes hanging tempting him
to one day ring the bells with power

then one quiet sunday morning
before the others had arrived
he quickly climbed the belfry stairs
and up a bell rope swiftly climbed

the clanging caught the priest off guard
and punishment he dealt the lad
the jesus poster other kids were given
altar boy did not get for being bad

the following week he was forgiven
and received the poster from the priest
he was told that god forgave him
but for altar boy this meant the least

as he grew older he became doubtful
that all of this had any meaning
he moved away from the myth
and saw it as mankind dreaming

he tried to make sense of how the world
the universe in its infinity
drove humans to invent explanations
seeking truth through absurdity

despite his abandoning religious myths
the altar boy recalled with gratitude
the priest and others who tried to help him
build a life of love and fortitude

TANKS

the first snow had fallen
when the soviet tanks rolled through
the small town
on the way to budapest
to crush the revolution
to slaughter civilians
who were demanding
the most basic of human rights
freedom from oppression and mistreatment

the young boy stood with his mother
by the side of the road
watching with naïve awe
and not understanding
but having heard
that these people
in uniforms in these huge machines
were going to hurt
other people like him and his family

he asked his mother
if he could make some snowballs
with rocks inside
and throw them at the soldiers
popped up from the tank turrets
suspiciously eying the crowd

he wondered if it would scare them
and make them go back
to where they came from
but his mother dissuaded him
saying that they would not go away
but would hurt all the people watching

so the young boy and his mother
went back into the house to prepare
for their imminent departure
from their homeland
to the west
to foreign places
to unknown realities
and hope of new lives
away from oppression and evil
sadly leaving their homeland behind

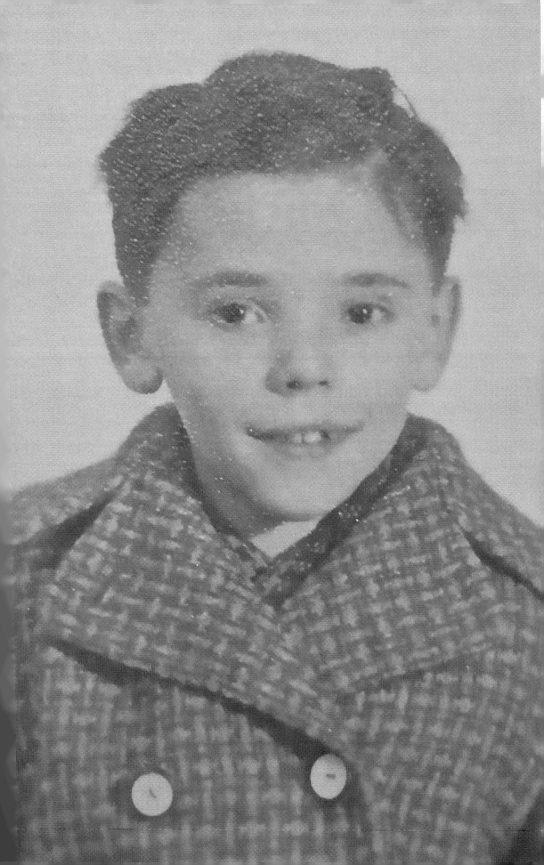

ZUCKER

after the soviet tanks
trundled through the town
they rolled on into budapest

buildings crumbled
civilians slaughtered
the revolution was crushed

in a few short days
mother sold or gave away
all worldly possessions

she packed one suitcase
dressed the boy and younger brother
in multilayers of clothes

they were going to visit grandma
is what mother told the boys just in case
the roaming secret service asked

train ride to a town in the west
then onto a small village even closer
to the austrian border

at the edge of town there was a soviet tank
soldiers checking anyone leaving
mother said they were visiting family on a farm

late at night mother paid the farmer
he was not family but he helped people escape
guiding them to where the iron curtain had been cut

they trudged along muddy fields
when flares went up they hit the ground
till the light went out and the gunfire stopped

a dense fog descended and the farmer guide
was concerned about finding the break
in the notorious iron curtain

two hours later the fog was lifting
a faint light emerged in the distance
the boy had pushed on with determination

and that is when it happened
he stepped upon a large paper sack
on which was the word zucker

zucker is german for sugar
and a few more hundred yards ahead was
the sweet austrian town of nickelsdorf

mother and boys were free
as they joined so many fleeing souls
in this ominous but hope-filled adventure\

REFUGEE KID

his heart was beating
faster and faster
his throat was dry
hands a bit shaky

first day of public school in england
age ten in a foreign land
barely speaking the language
leery of schoolmates
as they stared and scowled
with curious resentment wondering why
this refugee kid from another country
was allowed to be among them

the small shoves and shoulder bumps
communicated their feelings
toward this uninvited foreigner
till one day a feisty lad
put up his fists and challenged him
within minutes a circle of classmates formed
taunting and scoffing the refugee kid

the feisty one threw a couple of punches
as the circle of classmates jeered and cheered
but the refugee kid skillfully evaded the blows
and with one firm punch knocked feisty down
nose bleeding tears streaming
feisty was crushed and embarrassed

the cheering stopped as the circle receded
but the refugee kid bent down and said
"i sorry hit you"
catching feisty off guard as he tried to recover
and awkwardly allowing refugee kid
to help him stand up

the next day the refugee kid
gave feisty a chocolate bar
and though he was embarrassed
feisty accepted and quickly unwrapped it
broke it in two handing half to the refugee kid

the two became best friends for years
and taught the others
important life lessons about
forgiveness and acceptance
embracing two of the most
ignored essentials of humanity
if we are to survive together
on our pale blue dot

RUGBY

refugee kid starts grammar school
strict uniform code
and good behavior expectations

he is still learning about the culture
his english language improving
starting to get cautiously accepted

he surprises the teachers
as he excels in all subjects
ahead of the native classmates

despite some discomfort among faculty
and fellow students
he is treated with respect and acceptance

he learns the game of rugby quickly
as a fast runner and skillful dodger
scores for his team on several occasions

in addition to his academic achievements
he is made the captain of the rugby team
and respects the unique honor

the game he is most proud of
is when he and his friend were heading for a try
which is the same as a touchdown in american football

they are running fast and hard
evading tackles and grabs
and a few yards from the goal line

he passes the ball to his friend
who runs and touches the ball down
to score the winning points

the kid played many more games of rugby
and gained respect from classmates and staff
but he strived to pass on success to his teammates
because that is what he valued most
as a humble reflection of his own success

GUY FAWKES NIGHT

more than four hundred years ago
the gunpowder plot was averted
as guy fawkes was apprehended
guarding a huge collection of barrels
filled with gunpowder
under the english houses of parliament

to celebrate the successful prevention
of a major political catastrophe
the english celebrate guy fawkes night
with bonfires and fireworks displays

refugee kid and his friends gathered
around a huge pile of dry branches
ready for the flames to ascend
and ready to send their simple fireworks
in colorful displays up to the heavens

but it was a dank and cold evening
and the bonfire would not light
with all the crumpled papers
that his dad had gathered and lit

so in a risky and dangerous maneuver
to please the young lads
his dad hurled a full bucket of petrol
onto the flickering papers
and created a magnificent bonfire
that burned for a good long time

as the kid recalls this episode
in his early life
and adds his experience
as an emergency physician
in later life

he recognizes the amazing fortune
of his dad not going up in flames
all to please the kid and his friends

WHITE COATS

the students in the white coats
receive rigorous training in
   diagnosing
   treating
   prognosticating

but too often the curriculum
does not address the essentials of
   caring
   supporting
   empathizing

while medical schools
and residency programs
are getting better
they still have a way to go
to ensure that future doctors
understand and are able to grow

not just as diagnosticians
but as caring individuals
able to relate and understand
what their patients and families
are struggling with and going through

HEARTBEATS

one
two
three
four
five

HERE

the fetus is alive
with a chance to thrive
in its mother's womb
while waiting to arrive
how many heartbeats will follow
is undetermined and unpredictable
perhaps only ten thousand
or maybe over two billion more
whether dying shortly after birth
or as a centenarian at the farewell door
there are many reasons that heartbeats end
disease trauma violence suicide
starvation and combinations that
terminate each human life
regardless the last beats are all the same
the countdown is no different
whether a small gasping infant
or an elderly human with a fading frame

five
four
three
two
one

GONE

NEW LIFE

gravel dry tears
of animals and man
steal brief luxury
from time

flying bat tracks
through inky skies
to the past
soon
all gone

the rich
the destitute
equally away
into the ground
into the elements
to nurture new life

pristine air breezes over
bald heads of newborn infants
and other hatchlings
as crystal water
sprouts again
their future

their precious
new existence
on earth

PERCEPTION

if i could have solved
the problems in my life
i might have absolved
so much of my strife

could have would have
always the tenuous options

holding onto my perceptions
flawed as they may be
i so yearn for inclusions
to be among the free

but what is freedom after all
but an illusion
for we are all beholden
to the complexities of relationships
and our vague perception of our own

EXISTENCE

LIFE CHANGES

no matter how bad you feel
no matter how good it was
you will never be the same
or feel the same
as you did before

this keeps you going
        in a direction
        hoping
it is the right direction

never feeling as bad or as good
        as you felt before
        but different
        from the last pain
        from the last joy

EMBRACE

The ever-changing differences
the fluid nuances
from day to day
moment to moment
for this is what makes life

LIVABLE

SOMETIMES HAPPY

so many things in life
drive our happiness or strife
family connections
business rejections
friendly collaboration
workplace dilapidation
daddy loves mommy
who found another honey
kids had all they ever wanted
so now daddy is not needed

the spinning circle of life
is about happiness and strife

SOMETIMES HAPPY

SOMETIMES SAD

WATER OF LIFE

snail-slime warm-wet
sidewalks glistening
with suspended rain
laid down on the ground
like fractals of mist
make sparkling contours of
deck chairs and
picnic tables
on concrete house-skirts
frowzy wet cats
musty shivering dogs
shake large drops
from oleanders
on their tentative passage
for shelter
meeting water-shiny
distractions on the way
like slugs and black beetles
smelling familiar
now leaf-covered mounds
ruddy cheeked
kindergarten recess-people
in colorful rubber boots
trampling through
mud puddles
twirling round
water-pearl-covered
metal bars
as they babble and giggle
like children
born of rivers brooks and streams
making their way home
along shimmering sidewalks

INSIDIOUS

a short while ago
a little time past
not far hence
beyond a wormwood mast
a clown
a frown
a face
flat down
comes edging
onto
planked terraces
and seeps
into awakening minds with
octopus ink
darkening
shading
the dawn of a new day
to moderate
their expectations
and whims
of life

DENIGRATED LIFE

lip spelled maundering
by the guardians of society
on faux news
on special broadcasts
spill pseudo-moral vomit
and lies into living rooms
with killings of justice before
and revenge for murders of
maniacs thereafter

repeated numbing stimulus
raises the threshold of its perception
so we will soon be able
to tolerate crimes of anarchy
on our streets
under our windows
done unto our children
by the noxious offspring
of the tv addicted
self-proclaimed
guardians of society
denigrating the sanctity
and meaning of life

MISOGYNY

the way we evolved
as male and female
rendered the behaviors
that differentiated the genders

since females bore the offspring
they were by nature driven
to stay in the caves and make food
from the creatures the males
brought back from their hunts

yet even from the evidence
of these early humans
males and females had equal say
in the various aspects of their lives

over the millennia
the gender roles were gradually
contorted and twisted away
from the paleolithic levels of equality
even the biblical tale of the "creation"
revealed the pathetic misogynistic
absurdity of eve being created from
the rib of a male by a super dude
who clearly had no respect for her gender
or of what was up ahead regarding his
very bizarre maneuver

male dominance in many cultures
and diverse populations
increased over the millennia
until a time when females
rightly had enough of
subjugation and derision
though many nations today
are still ruled by toxic authoritarians that
treat females with disrespect and disregard
the times are moving beyond
these twisted male-dominated
ancient belief-driven norms

misogyny takes many forms
and should be deplored and rejected
we are all humans
we are all equal
we all demand respect
regardless of gender

misogyny has no place
in our society or any society
that wishes to survive and thrive
in this century or the beyond
on our pale blue dot

NEANDERTHAL INC

from cold dank caves
with fireless nights
the brutal stream of interaction
with self-proclaimed leaders
has changed very little
over the millennia

instead of physical abuse
smashing skulls with clubs
stabbing with sharp objects
there are brutally refined ways
of abusing and exploiting fellow humans
in the corporate setting

for far too many in leadership roles
the c-suite and board room
are now the cold caves
devoid of the comforts
of caring and support
for so many striving and struggling

the only difference now
suits and ties
incessant egotistical blabber
and always avoiding blame
and responsibility for failures
so these modern-day neanderthals
self-proclaimed leaders
can undeservedly ascend

but thankfully there are exceptions
as in days gone by
the exceptional good leaders
have self-awareness and authenticity
are respectful and honest
responsible and dependable

communicate with clarity
embracing flexibility

through these characteristics
and genuine behaviors
they motivate and elevate
their teams and organizations
to success and deserved recognition

LISTENING LEADERSHIP

st hual is the patron saint
of one of the key elements
of effective enlightened leadership

in addition to the other essentials
that are embraced by successful leaders
those who follow the guidance
and the recommendation of st hual
become the most respected and admired

st hual offers this guidance

simply and succinctly
with the letters that spell its name
st hual = shut the hell up and listen
highly recommended
by many fine leaders
who use it every day

MORE THAN GENIUS

beyond intellectual designation
numbers on special test scores
brilliant discoveries and dissertations
the brightest minds have often
remained humble and humbled
by the depth of their understanding
of our world and species

of our profound limitations
as human beings with such vast
divergence in
knowledge
intelligence
resourcefulness
physical capabilities
adopted belief systems
and perspectives on life

so many very advanced humans
have chosen to stay in the background
realizing the futility of challenging
fellow members of the species
on so many disturbing issues about life
and respecting their ability and fragility
to comprehend and accept the complexities

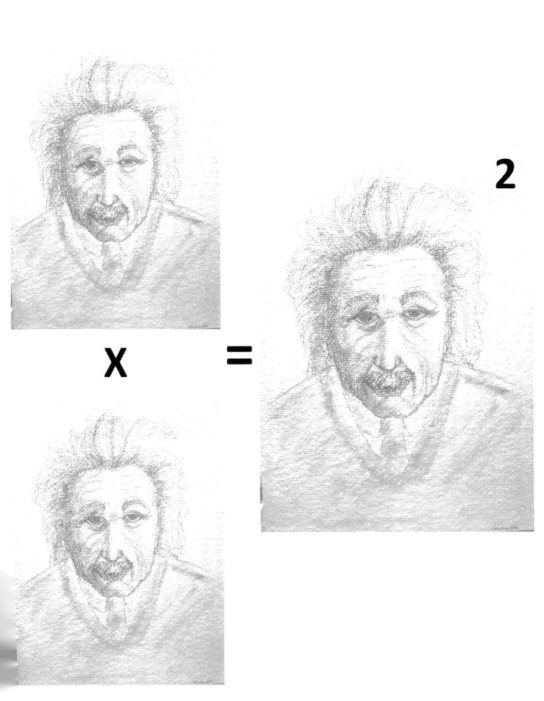

LIFE AND REALITY

as a member of the middle class
he is well
belly filled
suited housed and tanned
but his anxieties are many
and seem absurdly significant

the paint on the porsche is chipped
when to repaint
how much
what shade

his friend just bought
a seventy-five inch
QLED 8K full sun outdoor TV
he must get one soon

another friend vacationed in the Bahamas
he must go to tahiti this year
or maybe jamaica

his friend's bright son
attends an expensive private school
he must enroll his son tomorrow
in one that is better

but alas
if he lost everything
and ended up alone tomorrow
his anxieties would be few
and would seem small
on the scale of life and reality

he would only need
food
shelter

but then again
it is likely
he would be tempted
to dream
about a way back
to the middle class

ANOTHER NIGHTMARE SONG

thrashings with hoses and
rubber galoshes
beatings with big sticks
and lead-filled koshes

turns of the thumbscrews
rusty nose rings
these are a few of my
nightmare-laced things

when the whip cracks
when the neck creaks
when my agony is in vain

i think of
a few of my favorite things
so i can

SCREAM

…again

DRIVEN

if a mind can overflow
with the desire for knowledge
and the experiences of life
mine is mutinously driven
at many an inconvenient hour

driven to understand
the meaning
the significance
the mysteries
that so many seek

ABOUT LIFE

SECOND LIGHT

children of midnight
carry the bier
of yesterday's solemn tears
in flagons of gutted steel

cattle graze on cowslips
and grass of the dead
indifferently
not knowing who is below
hinders not their hunger

come away
from the embers
let them cool to ashes
for tormented wood
turns into gray powder

so the flames of life
will not survive
without
needs
wants
desires
like a flickering candle
in a breeze
one second
alight
and then
………

DID I LIVE?

i set the alarm on the clock
and pull the curtains closed
doors locked
windows secured
fading embers reminisce of the
evening's fire that once leapt in the hearth
like the fire that i once kept in my mind

i sleep tonight realizing that
my greatest accomplishments are incomplete
my love is shielded for fear of rejection
my pleasures all have boundaries
of control and condescension
doled out by others

i fear that i may not have
actually lived
but wasted air
and merely

EXISTED

REALITY?

tossed by the callused hand of fate
proscribed by an orbit and spin of brand
a unique peculiarity to each life
by laws of physics controlling
heaven and earth
disdaining faith and steadily moving
unfelt and unfeeling in its own dark ring
of reality
in perpetuity

regardless of our beliefs
desires or imagination
how do we know
that our lives are
driven by reality

since we cannot actually
define reality itself
and separate it from
mere perception

DIRECTION

i am drained of almost all
emotional energy
no longer do i know what i am feeling
i am in a mysterious limbo
that has me trapped
clambering through a spider's web
of complex feelings
that leave me directionless and unmotivated

but alas
i am not without hope
i am alive
i will survive
i need direction
hopefully in sight

i desire companionship
caring and kindness
but i don't need them
if i cannot have them

so be it
for i do not need anything
right now
but to feel the mere trembling of life

SURVIVAL

old men are killers
with their sanctity of years
wearing seniority
like tarnished medals
six star generals of life

time condones
their own lasting
in these frail vessels
whether bitter fools
or valiant veterans
their survival
vindicates them

but eventually they start to fade
and look to those
they loved and raised
for the merciful gestures
of understanding
gratitude and love

for so much of their lives
were given over the years
to their loved ones
with caring laughter and tears
passing along their inclination
to live life with determination
and love without reservation

they did this with no regrets
a relentless drive and attitude
and no need for gratitude

WHIM OF LIFE

i slept in the forest
and wept in a stream
chilled by winter thaw
i begged that with its motion
it calmed my woes
peculiar
invented
manufactured
fabricated
misconstrued
artificial

WOES

i implored that
as it rippled and flowed
it soothed the writhing cortex
with its unpredictable
yet calming motion
stirring the dead flesh
with the fresh death
of crumbled sunbaked leaves
begotten of massive life
beyond this ephemeral state
this whim
of my life
seeking wonders
far beyond my imagination

RECALLED

i don't want to be
the last bad thought recalled
nor some dredge of circumstance
at which to be appalled

let me be a free spirit
a breeze of life on your weary mind
something that once lost
you may again be pleased to find

MY LIFE

i sit
on a bench
on the rim of my life
all the stations
alleys
green fields
are behind me now

suckling
crawling
toddling as an infant
walking as a child
running as a youth
climbing as a man
learning
marrying
fathering

LEAVING

i have read and run
climbed and swum
skied and flown
wept and grown
but now i wait
and sit on a bench
while my life lingers on
soon to be gone

few will remember me
for my life as reality
in spite of senility
will be remembered only by

ME

WHY

as parents we
give and give
love and love
devote and sacrifice

we take pride
in what we thought
was the good result
of our endeavors

hoping that our children
learned and succeeded
engaged and connected
with our challenging world

yet there may be so much disconnect
with our beloved offspring
misunderstandings and misinterpretations

sadly and irrationally
these dear ones distanced those
who promoted them and helped them
learn about life as they struggled
with so many challenges

but now they are adults
who can choose whether they
want to remain connected with
the ones who helped them succeed
or fly free and leave their loved ones behind

some choose to stay connected
appreciating the love and support
and some need to move on

disconnecting
disconnecting
disconnecting

but not sure

WHY

LOVE

WHAT IS LOVE?

who can explain love
what is it
where did it come from
why is it
when did love
become an aspect of life

today we may define love
in many different ways
love among people
love of the natural world
love of the mystery that is life

but when did love become recognized
as a human emotion
that drives certain aspects
of human behavior

when cro-magnon and neanderthal
developed their primitive civilizations
did they have love that they only shared
with their own kind
did they even know about love
or was their version merely
animal protective instinct
no more emotional than
that of rats and racoons

with the evolution of species on the planet
there has been a redefining
perspective of love

there are several elements of love
that we humans have developed
defined and refined

over our stumbling evolution
respect
caring
kindness
devotion

but we still do not understand
why we have developed these concepts
driven by some mysterious emotions
triggered by various circuits in our brains
that have slowly and subtly
imprinted into our psyche
over the millennia

as we relate to our families and friends
perhaps it is irrelevant
or simply unimportant
to ponder how these
behavior-driven feelings
or
feelings-driven behaviors
became such a critical aspect
of our lives

perhaps we should just
accept
embrace
and love each other
regardless of differences in
ethnicity
politics
religion
capabilities
challenges

maybe this way
we can move to the next

mystery level of appreciating
what love is and how it can help
our human species survive
and thrive on our pale blue dot

OUR TRUE LOVE

impertinently constant
time
ferments the dew drops
of infatuation
on the sweet tenuous buds
of desire
till that subtle moisture
has nourished its awakening petals
to the bloom
of our true love

WITH YOUR LOVE

lest bewitched by the taunting
of past wretched days
let my mind be touched
by your gentle soul
and stay hooded
from the brazen glare
of the evil stealth
and foraging wit
of my history's cruel plight

see me
test me
let me
at your
peace be

slipping gently
into your mind
let me find
a place
in the race
out of pace

and in time
with your love
immune from
the mourning dove
will i be alive again

GO IF YOU MUST

i know i don't have any right to your heart
i know i can't have the grace of your love
but i can dream
of you and me
living far away
happy and free

i know i cannot
make you love me
though i want to be
with you every day

i want to hear your voice
and touch you
gently as an angel
yearning that you will
never go away

please tell me you would if you could
and i would relish that mere thought

and then

go if you must
and leave your soft loving smile
with me

BEYOND REPAIR

walking back over my shadow
wondering
how i could have
done things better
kinder and with more
understanding

i know i tried
in my own way
naïve and simple way
heartfelt and genuine
in effort and intent
but none of it was ever
received as intended

when a family is broken
repair is often too difficult
too complicated
with fracture lines
that will not mend
and will never heal

despite eager hearts
seeking reconciliation
the schisms and their history
are beyond repair
and there is little hope
to mend
or start afresh

LOVE AGAIN

one-legged katydid
lighted on the screen door
with a cheerful monophonic chirp

and a seven-legged spider
weaved its webs
perhaps categorized as "seconds"
or "irregulars" by some

a crippled little dog
limped and played happily
with all the other canine cripples

imperfect as i am
with all my incapacities
foolishness and emotional infirmities

i ask you
to let me start
to love you again

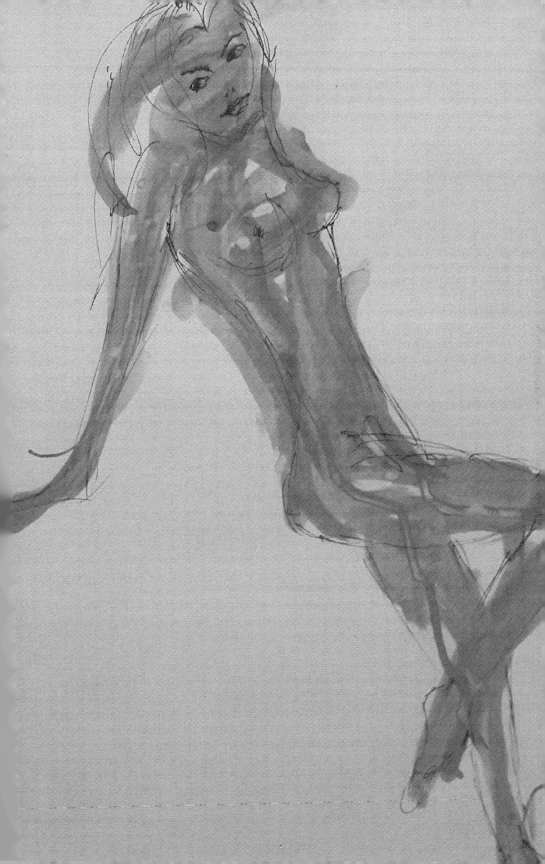

TEMPTRESS

a weary soul am i
peaceless days
spent in languid seclusion

walls and lamps
are my companions now
years of unfulfilled dreams
are my past

a calm amidst
confusion
sleeps
waits
in days
in nights

but soon
it will placate
the restless heart

pass not over a sincere mind
cautious but eager
wounded yet whole
waiting
for the kind presence
and gentle strength
of a temptress
to life

LOVE DANCED

peaceful eyes of onyx set
in crinkled smiles of satin
ochre skin
soft and yielding
yet the hopeful glimmer of love
not let in

a lighthouse beam in passion's fog
guiding intents to veering trails
i cling to its strength in lusting's bog
but its ephemeral limb my loving fails

love has played and danced with me
sidling to my frailty
truing my obliquity
a sacred place
without holy sanity
intangible graces
and wretched sanctity

laurels on my faithless head
all is not lost when love departs
love is extant in sincere hearts
and is not gone with our beloved dead

RESCUE ME

the tormented strings
of my frustrated mind
painfully taut
stretched to snap
moved by the smallest
wisps of bitter wind
to a baleful wailing
cacophony
of anguish

as though its true intent
unable to express
it flounders
on grit beds of
unrealistic possibilities
stumbling
from one small hope of life
to another

its wretched state
mollified by false hopes
of future love
of contentment to come
of new life

but now reaping the sour fruits
of a green mad escape
i languish
in doldrums of an unfeeling

SENSE

unaware of awareness

LOST

in a small place of
purposelessness
hopelessness

RESCUE ME
(if you will)

strip off the constraints
of unfulfillment
so that i may find
the goal of my true modest desire
in the deep strength
of your warm
singular

LOVE

HER REGRET

now she begins her
new life
on the financial gains
from her departed former mate

but alas
it dawns on her
doubting mental faculties
that in spite of all
the money
and the plastic fun
life is not the same
not quite complete
without him

SOMETIMES

sometimes it's tempting
 not to get up
  not to care
   not to want to live

when the pain is just too much
 from grief
  from separation
   from alienation

but not getting up is not an option
 for life
  for caring
   for love

so, i must just get it together and
 live
  care
   love

because that is all there is…

HMM

after tea
i meet with thee
hocus pocus
hullaballoo
there went a black cat
and i got you

LOSS

MOTHER

FATHER

MOTHER

her son awakens on sheets
that were her sails
filled with the lusty breath of life

he sees her face
on other faces
in other faces

he smells her fragrant presence
in acacia breezes
and orange blossoms

he sees her soft eyes
in the edge of a still winter night
full of life yet
full of sadness
tender loving brown eyes
that seemed to presage the agonies
that would torment her

he sees her mouth
whose smiles
were kisses
and whose anger
was love

he remembers well
her sweet blind innocence
crushed crumbled
like the petals of a crisp dry rose
whose form though gone
is brought to mind
by the gentle fragrance
left behind
so he recalls

the innocence
the love
the grace
and how these virtues
blessed his dear

MOTHER

FATHER

he was raised by a simple mother
who had little schooling
and who had to deal with
hate and derision
cast her way

he was raised by a loving mother
who relentlessly drove on
after her husband
unexpectedly died
leaving her behind
to fend for herself
and a toddler

early on
the young lad
did not understand
how fortunate he was
to have such a mother
who loved and cared so much

later he realized
that he survived and thrived
because of her strength
and devotion to his success

inspired and driven
by her selfless caring
he became a doctor
and a patriot for his nation

he married an angel
and saved his family
from soviet oppression
creating new lives for them

in western worlds

over his selfless caring life
he helped so many
he healed so many
he saved so many

his heart of gold
though shrouded
with sad memories
always glowed
with kindness and love

and when he was finally ready
to leave our pale blue dot
he knew that the very best
he had offered
would help his beloved
to succeed
just as his dear mother
helped him
saved him

indeed the altar boy
the refugee kid succeeded
because of the virtues and kindness
passed along to him by his dear

FATHER

BOY

squirming and struggling
reality is fading
the toddler lies in bed
doctors have no idea
what is up ahead

bloody urine and fading brain
has the clinicians puzzled
no such condition is known
at this time in medicine

despite his dark prospect
of recovery and survival
his mind and body are not ready
to leave
so he fights hard and

RECOVERS

as with so much unknown in medicine
the toddler has a condition
to be later identified and named
hemolytic uremic syndrome

HUS

so this fragile toddler
gradually recovers
with basic medical support
and his beloved parents

FAST FORWARD

the boy is now a doctor
caring for a young girl with hus
her kidneys shut down
her brain shuts down

the doctor does all that is possible
to save the little angel
but death silently has its way
hearts break for the family and

DOCTOR

ANOTHER ANGEL LEAVES

she first came to the doctor
when she was two years old
diagnosed with leukemia

tests were reviewed
with mom and dad
treatment plans were set

chemotherapy started
frequent office visits
for testing and treatment

the parents were trusting
they adored their sweet angel
struggling and trying to survive

the final treatments completed
moving onto observation
testing and monitoring

for two years there was hope
prayers were answered
and the sweet angel thrived

but then the blood beast returned
with even greater vengeance
requiring more aggressive treatment

after several options had been tried
there were none left that would help
the little angel to survive

parents and doctor were heartbroken

and the options for the end
were empathetically addressed

mom and dad took their daughter home
with medicine to quell her increasing pain
doctor visited the family to help them
through the painful ordeal

the sweet angel passed peacefully
cradled by mother and father
till her last sweet angel breath

PLAY

rippled trees and marble skies
gnats are specks around my eyes
grey chimney smoke i smell
swirling into heaven or hell
but neither exists in reality's well
screech owls fester the air with noise
frogs by limpid pools are poised
away dreary day
hail weary night
for dreams of children
playing with angels
is now my only flight

LET IT BE

i limp and lisp from life's torments
a wretched creature of fate am i
a fate of my own devising
methinks

how keen the edges
of life's wasted shards
how heavy the leaden weights
of past regrets

now melting in the warm sun
yearning for newfound life and love
a piteous creature
of its own destruction
am i

perhaps i should leave
now
and let the world
be

BUTTERFLY WINGS

i sleep with sallow gargoyles
and wan seething gorgons
skidding on the ice moon
breathing hot running tar
puking on yellow butterfly wings

constraints of time
bring dreams
from wakeful reality
for a while

but the monster of night
the salacious creature
of morphea
ever subtly
spikes the eyes
with chips of ice moon
and drops of tar

and when i see butterfly wings
in anguish
i painfully wish
to be awake
again

TERMINAL

one hour passed
unceasing, valiant measures
were taken
but he died
anyway

he was famous
wealthy
a social climber
near the top
of the everest of hedonism
but then he could have been a philanthropist
or an engineer
or an addict on skid row
or you

dead
is the only and ultimate state of
unity and uniformity

the fly you swat today
is no less dead
than you may be
tomorrow

THE MAILMAN

mrs price just killed the mailman
turning into her driveway
she didn't see his shiny motorcycle
as he was flying on his mail delivery quest
blue federal rags

EXPLODED

the doc resuscitated the mailman
admitted him to the icu
but due to the extent of his injuries
he died two days later

though she innocently never conceived
this end to a fellow human being
mrs price just killed the mailman

the doc feels deeply
for the mailman and his family
but as much for mrs price for
her grief and sadness

BOMB TECH

his young heart pounding
the bomb tech sees the wires
attached to cold sleek grey metal
covered with rubble
buckled rags tins broken glass
and the dust of generations
ancient family lines
inscrutable
seething
here now
for a roaring
deadly second

A FLASH

fractured organs
seared flesh
splintered limbs
burnt lidless eyes
fountain scatter
in a hideous death plume
brother son husband father
knowingly willing prepared

TO DIE

small pieces
in a box
a dead hero
escorted by one
saluted by few
unknown to many
the family cries
but now

HE IS HOME

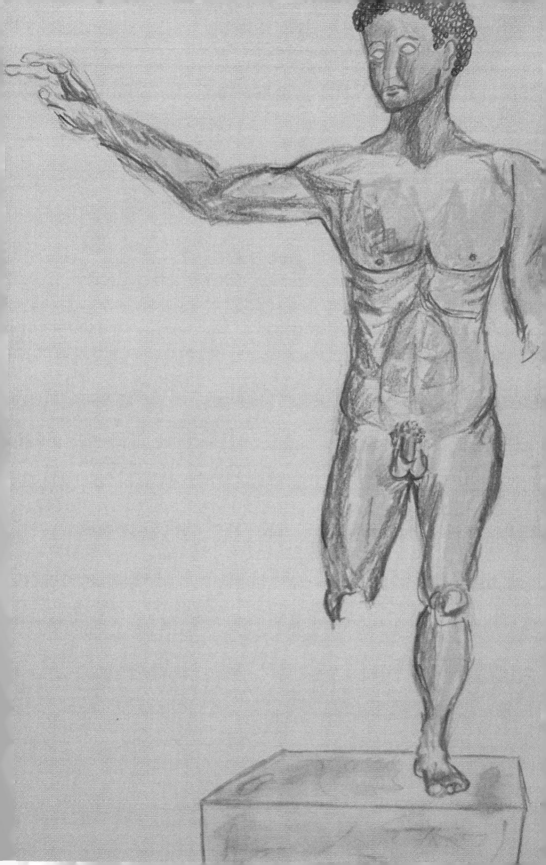

THE HERO

cold wind swirls
crisp brown leaves
on miles of marble floors

icy echoes
silenced by the air
between white walls

the hero saved others
and sacrificed his life
for theirs

now he wanders aimlessly
among the ivory pillars
calling but not hearing
his own voice

the sound merely turns
to snow blowing down
long halls of crystal quartz
disappears in a panoply of light

movement turns to geometric form
time is
life is not
in the infinite time space
of his death

GOODBYE

pale grey skins of eucalyptus trees
on cut ivy leaves --- beneath
stucco boxes
barbecue smoke-blackened
rough-sawn cedar eaves --- above
pin-striped car flanks
bronze-oiled skin
of taut thighed mindless youth --- beside
surfboard blister footed
gold chain embraced necks
bored pickup drivers
continental chauffeurs --- around

the nightmares of the pleasure getter
the fantasies of something better
i try to escape
crawl out
of the mesmerizing
sewer of hedonism
through shrinking manholes of sanity
through slim crevices of reality
breaking away
cutting loose
from the tentacles
holding me subtly
in the dream
i once thought that i wanted
but i must leave
while i am still sane
before it is too late
my simplicity to retain

OUR FATHERS

the treacheries of

CIVILIZATION

electronic-nuclear-automatic-power-windows on life
plush-plastic-machined-smooth-comforts
pampering
embracing
insidiously suffocating
the hidden embers
of primitive innocence
within the dying soul
of man's inner

SANCTUM

Yet another prayer:

our fathers
forgotten are thy names
we have given you
our daily ignominy
but forgive us naught
for we will lead our children
from the knowledge of you
to dazzling defilement and hatred
so, we really don't need you
aye men

the past dies
in the eclectic pleasures
of the present and the future
zapped-kerpowed-zoomed
into emptiness
gone with each dying
ignorant being
who knew nothing

history dies
murdered by thoughtless passions
of the empirical present
and the dubious

UNKNOWN

NO BUSINESS HERE

princes and paupers
reapers and hawkers
all come out at night and see
their feeble frame's humanity

for 'ere they lay on sheets of satin
sackcloth hay or wooden slatting
their spirits floated free in space
no torso arms legs or face

but now they are bound
in one place to be found
daily fettered to flesh and bone
not seeing together they are alone

alone at the mercy of their twisted minds
wherein passion anxiety and fear they wind
a macabre sequence of painful events
and not till death do they repent

life is not life nor death the end
reality is pretense the mind it bends
with rules and logic of its own creation
from family units to all the nations

alas soon 'twill all be over
the present gone and spirits sober
we all will "fly" beyond the stratosphere
for we really have no business here

HOPE?

WHAT IS HOPE?

just like love
hope is an inscrutable
element of human existence

when our aboriginal predecessors
were merely trying to survive
did they have hope
of anything in their minds
of any circumstances
in their primitive existence

how did the neurons and synapses
in their brains
develop such a force
that has driven individuals
and populations
to act in small
and universal ways
to perpetually move
our stammering development
as human beings
in our minimally relevant
existence in the vastness of the

UNIVERSE

through hope

EVERY DAY

every day brings hope anew
for family friends and for you

celebrate life while you are here
do not embrace doubt and fear

for this life is all that we really know
and one day we will all have to go

so make each day a time to grow
for all those that you love and know

a good heart will always follow
this genuine path today and tomorrow

TOGETHER

so many times as humans
we have questioned our own
irrationality
stupidity
cruelty

yet we have no answers
no rational corrections
only weird observations about
historical documentation of
tribes that murdered each other
civilizations that slaughtered each other

from cro-magnon and neanderthal conflicts
to millennia of hominids
slaughtering each other
over basic survival needs
and invented mythologies

now we have governments
driving their military to slaughter
ensuring that they are uplifting
and inspiring their unique rationale
and "logic" for all actions
going back to the early days
of cro-magnon and neanderthal
engagement over the most
basic differences should never
lead to death for our own species
at the hand of our own species

so many wonder and hope
that this thinking
or lack of thinking
may stop so that we humans
may all embrace survival
and rational engagement

we can do this
because we have hope
for a better world
with understanding
compassion and caring
for all our fellow humans

we must embrace each other
regardless of mythological beliefs
despite differences
physical
intellectual
emotional

if we can connect
with our human complexities
regardless of our differing views
on so many aspects of life
we should be able to survive
and thrive together with

HOPE

HUMANS

white
beige
brown
black
yellow
short
tall
slender
plump
learning
learned
challenged
challenging

WE ARE ALL HUMANS

to survive
we must strive
for the same basic
values
goals
outcomes

through
caring
kindness
compassion
love

over millennia
we have evolved
from wild bipeds
who slaughtered
each other for food
to arrogantly self-proclaimed

advanced civilizations that
rebuke the basic principles
and ideals of civilization
caring
kindness
compassion
love

we now slaughter
in the name of mythologies
pretense of salvaging
the beliefs about life
held by artificially
defined groups
divided by
thousands of languages
evolved cultural norms
delusions of superiority

but in the end
we are humans
risking life
inanely driven
by artificial principles
egomaniacal leaders
who persuade
the vulnerable
the gullible
to be believers
to risk their lives
and the survival of humanity
on our pale blue dot

let us move beyond
irrationality to enlightenment
embracing the only tenets
of our future survival
caring
kindness
compassion
love

SINCERE

reconsider stability
to replace it with a free life
for there is only
one spin shake and toss
in the complex game of existence
consider not embracing
deceptive pleasures
tangible banal amenities
materialistic mindless must-haves
yearnings for security

loosen the ties
sever the bindings
slip off the noose
of an insipid life
without the wit of imagination
without virtues sorrows and honest laughter
without the real person behind the hand-me-down mask

instead
cut the ropes of your one-time balloon
drift
float
over
through
new adventures
pursuing
the spectacle
the reality
the joy
of a sincere
original life of

HOPE

DARING

once i dared
once i tried
once i failed
tried again
failed again
tried again and again
failed again and again

then one time
because i continued
to try and strive
i succeeded

my dare became reality
caring
kindness
love
compassion
these are my parting labels
wherever i may go
hoping
that others will follow
and choose to be
caring
kind
loving
compassionate

because we all need
these four elements
of humanity
to thrive
to feel alive
to survive

MAY EVENING

skittering wind on duckless ponds
and childless pools of muddy water

squinted eyes as
streetlight stars
twinkle
chattering
to low heavy
listening clouds

dust-covered oranges
brown-tinged limp leaves
of late cool winter days

now gently rinsed
with the tepid drizzle
of an early may evening

as i venture out
into the fresh innocent world
around me
glimmers of life
and hope
surround me

HOPE AT THE END

what hope is there
without belief in some mysterious
wonderful something hereafter

the many belief systems
all have some hope to offer
to defray the reality of death
and the perception
of its frightening dark terminality

those who believe in their mythologies
embrace and carry a hope to their
fading minds as they take their last breath

but there is no less comfort
in accepting that after death
there is just nothing nonexistence

for we all did not exist before we were conceived
and after we die we will not exist for the second time
even though we may wonder
if it is indeed the last time

DEDICATION

These musings, mutterings, and mind meanderings are dedicated to my dear Chinese angel-wife, who gives me hope, healing and happiness.

She has made only one life demand of me, that I live to 130 years of age, and I am committed to giving that a solid Mad Hungarian effort.

ABOUT THE AUTHOR

Csaba was born a few years after the end of the second World War in Szeged, Hungary. His father Zoltan grew up in Transylvania, which was formerly a part of Hungary. Zoltan grew up struggling, along with 1.5 million Hungarians after World War I, when the region was taken over by the oppressive Romanian government.

With love and profound dedication, Zoltan's widowed, impoverished mother supported his passion and drive to become a physician. During World War II, Zoltan was a physician in the Hungarian military that was pushed forward by the Nazi regime acting as its front line of attack into Russia. He was an inspiration to the many young, inexperienced soldiers and saved many lives during the war.

As World War II was ending, the German military destroyed key locations as they retreated through Hungary, while the Russian forces added to the destruction in their efforts to push through Hungary to defeat the Nazi regime. It was under these circumstances that Zoltan ended up in Szeged, in southern Hungary and became a leading trauma surgeon in the city's largest hospital.

It was during these difficult times that Zoltan met Klara during a modest debutante event, when many struggling families were hoping to find a caring life companion for their daughters. Klara was a very bright and talented young actress and singer, and was recognized nationally for her talents. However, all of that had been suppressed during the brutal times of war and its aftermath.

After getting to know each other over a few months, Zoltan proposed to Klara, and although she was much younger than Zoltan, her family gave their blessing and the two of them were married.

Just over a year later, their first son was born, whom they named Csaba, after the youngest son of Attila the Hun. Csaba became a popular name for newborns as a rebuke by Hungarians to the oppression and mistreatment by the authoritarian communist regime, as a satellite nation of the Soviet Union.

Csaba was a feisty infant and needed plenty of attention and corrections. During his second year of life, Csaba became very ill and was hospitalized with a medical problem that would not be identified till decades later: hemolytic uremic syndrome. He received intensive care services, and his parents were warned that he may not survive. But because he was named after Prince Csaba, who never lost a battle, that most certainly was not going to happen!

At the age of seven, he escaped with his mother and younger brother, fleeing to Austria in the middle of the night, as the Soviets crushed the 1956 Hungarian revolution with an iron fist. Zoltan, Csaba's father, had left earlier to prepare for what was to come. The family was reunited in Austria and were accepted on the British refugee quota in early 1957.

A shy, self-conscious introvert, Csaba did his best to learn the new language and the customs of his peers in elementary school. He was ridiculed early on and ended up in a couple of fights with students who passed along their parents' resentment of the Hungarian refugees, the so-called state supported foreigners.

Csaba passed the Eleven-plus examination in the last year of primary school, which allowed him admission to an all-boys grammar school. Uniforms, strict behavior codes, and rigorous academic expectations were the norms in British grammar schools.

Csaba was keen to comply and succeed academically. After the first year, he was a topper among the 90 or so fellow students in academic standing, greeted with a certain mix of admiration and underlying resentment by students and teachers alike.

Meanwhile, having passed the required certification examinations for foreign physicians entering the country, Zoltan had become head of emergency medical services and trauma surgery at the hospital in their hometown of Caerphilly in South Wales. However, ultimately, Zoltan was not pleased with the way the healthcare system functioned in the UK and made the decision to take on private practice in Saskatchewan, Canada.

Csaba's mother had struggled with mental health issues over the years and would be absent from home for several days at a time. It was during one of these absences that Zoltan and Szabolcs, Csaba's younger brother, headed off to Canada, leaving Csaba by himself, at the age of 15, so he could finish out the school year.

A few days later, Klara came back home and was in bad shape. Csaba took care of her, cooked, and cleaned the home-and of course, did his schoolwork. Finally, he made the decision not to finish the school year, but to join his father and brother in Canada. Csaba's mother and he went to London to get passport updates and visa clearances - within a week, they were in the air, flying to Canada.

Since they arrived late in the school year, Csaba learned that he could challenge grade 12 subjects by passing the final exam. He arduously studied at home and successfully passed the exams.

The following year, while away at boarding school, his mother committed suicide. This was her second attempt and she succeeded, leaving behind a crushed family who had loved her so much, even during her challenging times with erratic behavior.

Even as he struggled with trying to understand and deal with his mother's demise, he drove on in his studies. He continued an accelerated academic path and completed his premedical degree, entering medical school at the age of 18.

He married at the age of 19. His wife and he had two boys during medical school in Loma Linda, California. After an internship in pediatrics, his wife and he divorced, but Csaba stayed close to his family, making sure he stayed connected with his two boys. Csaba worked as an emergency medicine physician and two years after his wife and him divorcing, they remarried. That lasted for four years, and they divorced again.

Csaba moved to Toronto, Canada, where he completed his pediatric training and also completed his pediatric hematology oncology fellowship. He married a pediatric oncology nurse and after finishing his fellowship, they moved together to California, where Csaba joined a multispecialty medical practice.

A baby boy joined Csaba and his wife during their first year back in California. However, at nine months of age, the infant developed a serious, unidentified illness and died two days later. Recovering from this traumatic episode in their lives, Csaba's wife and he had two more healthy baby boys and raised them together.

During the time raising the two lads from the second marriage, Csaba practiced pediatrics and pediatric hematology oncology in several settings: multispecialty clinic, solo practice, and finally in a staff model clinic in Southern California, where he held a number of executive level clinical leadership positions. Csaba worked as a senior leader in various healthcare industry settings and in a number of consulting roles. His goal has always been to improve healthcare services to the people being served.

Csaba's father, Zoltan, married many years after Klara's suicide. Zoltan lived in Canada with his second wife for twenty years, where he did solo practice as a family physician and surgeon. One morning, when his wife drove to work, after she got out of her car, she collapsed with a massive stroke and had to be put on life support.

Based on previous agreements they had made, under these circumstances, she did not want to be maintained on life support and wanted to donate her organs to patients who needed them. Seven people benefited from her decision.

Zoltan was profoundly impacted by this heart-wrenching event in his life and came down to California, where he lived with Csaba and his family for a year. Csaba and Zoltan worked on a similar arrangement as with Zoltan's wife, except for organ donation , due to his age not being appropriate as a donor.

Over the next three years, Csaba closely supported Zoltan during his dear father's steady decline into a deep state of Alzheimer's dementia and kidney failure until his ultimate, inevitable demise.

Csaba had previously taken his mother's ashes back to Hungary to be united in a family columbarium. Zoltan had no family left in Europe, so Csaba buried his ashes next to a magnificent Douglas fir in Forest Park, in Portland, Oregon, along with the ashes of his organ donor wife.

Csaba and his family moved to Portland, Oregon, where Csaba was a physician leader at two health insurance companies. When their two boys were teenagers, his second wife and he divorced. After yet another painful life experience, Csaba decided not to get back into the complicated interpersonal relationship space of marriage, and decided to just stay single.

That lasted for two years and he finally decided, in atypical form, to try something different. Csaba always had a great admiration for China, after having watched a brilliant ten-part British series called The Heart of the Dragon. So, he found the most secure online dating site for international relationships and dated his present Chinese wife for a year, with several visits to China and adventures with her all over the country. He facilitated his wife's immigration to the US on a fiancé visa and in January 2007, two weeks after she and her 12-year-old daughter arrived, they were married. Their respect and love for each other continues to grow and flourish.

After living in Portland for almost ten years, Csaba and his family moved down to Orange County, Southern California. Over the past six years, Csaba has worked as a physician reviewer, medical director, consultant and medical advisor.

Just as he was in his younger years, Csaba remains an overachiever due to a healthy dash of obsessive-compulsive disorder mixed with being an introvert who is not looking for praise. Nevertheless, over the years, Csaba has had a number of recognitions, which he accepted with humility and a dash of embarrassment.

In his third year of medical school, he was honored to become a member of the **Alpha Omega Alpha Medical Honor Society.** He has been a **MENSA** member since 1977. He was a **Malcolm Baldrige National Examiner** for three years and attended the recognition ceremonies presented by the Secretary of Commerce and POTUS. He was named **Clinician of the Year by CIGNA** and also recognized for his Physician Partnership on the health insurance side of the company. CAMBIA Health Solutions presented him with the highest recognition for his leadership, and the impact it had on the healthcare company's performance and reputation.

In addition to working in the healthcare industry, Csaba has always been driven by creating stories that have relevance in our current society. He has written several screenplays with social issue themes and finally produced a movie, **Here Awhile**, that portrays end-of-life empowerment.

The poems in Csaba's book are his reflections on the complexities of many events, feelings, and dreams over the decades of his life. Drawn from his experiences as a refugee, foreigner, physician, husband, father, teacher, and humble student of life, Csaba presents his observations on an expansive, complex and emotional journey.

Key drivers of these poems are issues with which Csaba has struggled over the years, as well as plenty of positive and inspiring experiences. Separation, disconnection, rejection, and the death of loved ones are issues balanced by inspiration, devotion, caring and unconditional love along the way.

Csaba has referred to himself as The Mad Hungarian: mad about life and all its messy complications; mad about all the goodness, caring and love he has encountered along the way- and mad about trying to understand and empathize with the struggles and losses that so many people experience in their lives on our pale blue dot.

You can learn more about Csaba through his website csabamera.com or follow his social media accounts accounts to stay updated about what The Mad Hungarian is thinking!

Instagram: csabathemadhungarian

Facebook: Csaba The Mad Hungarian

Musings of A Mad Hungarian